The BIG SNUGGLE-UP

For Linda and Tony - B.P.

For Laura and Felix - N.B.

First published in Great Britain in 2011 by Andersen Press Ltd.,
20 Vauxhall Bridge Road, London SW1V 2SA.
Published in Australia by Random House Australia Pty.,
Level 3, 100 Pacific Highway, North Sydney, NSW 2060.
Text copyright © Brian Patten, 2011.
Illustration copyright © Nicola Bayley, 2011.
The rights of Brian Patten and Nicola Bayley to be identified as the
author and illustrator of this work have been asserted by them in
accordance with the Copyright, Designs and Patents Act, 1988.
All rights reserved.
Colour separated in Switzerland by Photolitho AG, Zürich.
Printed and bound in Singapore by Tien Wah Press.
Nicola Bayley has used crayon in this book.

10   9   8   7   6   5   4   3   2   1

British Library Cataloguing in Publication Data available.
ISBN 978 1 84939 208 2
This book has been printed on acid-free paper

The BIG Snuggle-up

Brian Patten & Nicola Bayley

ANDERSEN PRESS

I asked a scarecrow in out of the snow,
"Please be a guest in my house."
The scarecrow said, "Can I bring a friend,
For in my sleeve lives a mouse?"

Into the house and out of the snow
Came a mouse and an old scarecrow.

A butterfly said, "Is it far too late
For me to come in and hibernate?"

Into the house and out of the snow
Came a butterfly, a mouse, and an old scarecrow.

A robin peeped out from its freezing nest,
"Would you mind if you had another guest?"

Into the house and out of the snow
Came a robin, a butterfly,
a mouse, and an old scarecrow.

A squirrel scampered down from a sycamore tree,
"I'll bring some nuts, if you'll shelter me."

Into the house and out of the snow
Came a squirrel, a robin, a butterfly, a mouse,
and an old scarecrow.

Next a sweet old rabbit with nowhere to go
Begged to be let in out of the snow.

Into the house and out of the snow
Came a rabbit, a squirrel, a robin,
a butterfly, a mouse,
and an old scarecrow.

A cat allowed itself to be let in
And it slept on a shelf by a blue bread bin.

Into the house and out of the snow
Came a cat, a rabbit, a squirrel,
a robin, a butterfly, a mouse,
and an old scarecrow.

Next came a dog. It had shaggy hair.
It made itself at home in a comfy chair.

Into the house and out of the snow
Came a dog, a cat, a rabbit, a squirrel,
a robin, a butterfly, a mouse,
and an old scarecrow.

A lamb and a fawn who were lonely and lost
Longed to come in and out of the frost.

Into the house and out of the snow
Came a lamb, a fawn, a dog, a cat, a rabbit,
a squirrel, a robin, a butterfly, a mouse,
and an old scarecrow.

A donkey looked in and said,
"I'm unable
To find my way back and into
the stable."

Into the house and out of the snow
Came a donkey, a lamb, a fawn, a dog, a cat, a rabbit,
a squirrel, a robin, a butterfly, a mouse,
and an old scarecrow.

"The lake," said the heron,
"is covered in ice.
Can I stand in the bath?
It would be nice!"

Into the house and out of the snow
Came a heron, a donkey, a lamb, a fawn, a dog, a cat,
a rabbit, a squirrel, a robin, a butterfly, a mouse,
and an old scarecrow.

Soon into the room sneaked a young fox.
"Can I doze by the fire in a hat-box?"

Into the house and out of the snow
Came a fox, a heron, a donkey, a lamb,
a fawn, a dog, a cat, a rabbit, a squirrel,
a robin, a butterfly, a mouse,
and an old scarecrow.

The owl swooped down silent and slow,
Shaking off flakes of frozen snow.

Into the house and out of the snow
Came an owl, a fox, a heron, a donkey, a lamb,
a fawn, a dog, a cat, a rabbit, a squirrel,
a robin, a butterfly, a mouse,
and an old scarecrow.

And we were all cosy, snuggled up warm
And we listened all night to a terrible storm.

And everyone agreed how nice it would be
To stay in that little warm house with me.